A FAIRY CALLED HILARY

A Fairy
Called Hilary

Linda Leopold Strauss

illustrated by Sue Truesdell

Holiday House/New York

This story first appeared in
Cricket, The Magazine for Children
from September 1995–January 1996.

Library of Congress Cataloging-in-Publication Data
Strauss, Linda Leopold.
A fairy called Hilary / Linda Leopold Strauss; illustrated by
Susan G. Truesdell.—1st ed.
p.   cm.
Summary: A fairy named Hilary comes to stay with Caroline and uses
her magic to enliven trick-or-treating on Halloween, the making of
a giant snowman, a friend's party, an airplane trip,
and a garden show.
ISBN 0-8234-1418-3
[1. Fairies—Fiction.   2. Magic—Fiction.]   I. Truesdell, Susan G., ill.
II. Title.
PZ7.S91245Fai   1999   [Fic]—dc21   98-19820   CIP
                                                                    AC

To Bill, Nancy, Katie, and all Hilary's
other friends who have been waiting and waiting.
L. L. S.

To Abby, with love.
S. T.

Contents

A FAIRY CALLED HILARY

1

Hilary Appears

I can hardly believe it myself now, that a fairy came to live with us when I was younger. We weren't allowed to talk about it at the time, except to one another. Hilary asked us not to.

We were on our way to the Natural History Museum when Hilary arrived that Sunday. I had just asked Daddy if he believed in fairies. He said no, which didn't surprise me.

Mother thought for a moment before answering.

"I don't think fairies are real, Caroline," she said, "but I believe in them."

And I knew just what she meant, because I felt exactly the same way.

At that very moment, a light breath of air, smelling delightfully of someplace else, blew softly across my face—and there Hilary was, sitting beside me. Daddy and Mother didn't notice her at first.

"Who are you?" I whispered.

"I'm Hilary," she whispered back. "A fairy. May I go to the museum too?"

Just like that. One minute the seat beside me was empty, and the next, there was Hilary. If you think I had trouble believing my eyes, imagine what happened when my father glanced into the rearview mirror and discovered Hilary in the backseat.

The problem was, Hilary didn't look like a fairy. She appeared to be about my age, with a wise little face and very ordinary, wispy brown hair. She wore a blue jumper with fuzzy dark red tights and sturdy brown shoes that were scuffed at the toes. I wanted to look and see

if she had wings tucked away somewhere behind her, but I was afraid of appearing impolite.

Daddy had no such fears. He simply and flatly refused to accept that Hilary was a fairy. I must confess I half agreed with him, because I was secretly thinking that if fairies did exist, they wouldn't look anything like Hilary. Still, she had appeared in the car out of nowhere; I was sure of that. But I was also sure Daddy would never believe it.

Mother, meanwhile, had turned to Hilary.

"You must understand, dear," she was saying, "that it's not that we don't want to believe you. But your parents must be worried. Don't you think we had better help you find them?"

"No, ma'am," replied Hilary. "No one's worrying about me, because they sent me here. So please, may we go to the museum?"

Mother looked a little taken aback. "Who sent you here?" she asked. "And—why?"

"Fairies have *always* lived with humans," Hilary said, seemingly surprised at the question. "Not all of us can come, of course, but there are always some of us around. And it's only for a visit. Not forever. It can never," she repeated thoughtfully, "be forever."

Daddy pulled the car to the side of the road abruptly. I could tell his patience was giving out because his eyebrows were going into that scowl that usually meant big trouble.

"This is ridiculous," Daddy said in a tone that sounded calm but really wasn't at all. "Do you know how ridiculous this is? Here we are, talking to this child about fairies, when what

4

we should be thinking about is finding her parents.

"Now then," he said, looking directly at Hilary. "Let's have it straight. Whom do you belong to, and how did you get in this car?"

"I appeared," said Hilary meekly.

Daddy's face got red. "I know you appeared, for heaven's sake," he retorted. "That's the whole problem! And I'm beginning to wish you'd *dis*appear!"

"I will," said Hilary, "but if you don't mind, I'll be back in five minutes." And instantly she was gone.

Daddy's mouth opened and stayed open. Mother put a reassuring hand on his arm. I looked all around the backseat, but there wasn't very far to look. There was no doubt about it. Hilary was gone.

"Oh, Daddy!" I wailed. There I'd been, with a chance to get to know a real live fairy, and now she had vanished.

"Well, thank goodness," said Daddy. "I don't know what's been going on here, but it seems to be over. Shall we catch our breaths for a minute and then go on?" He took out his handkerchief and wiped his forehead.

"No one will believe this," he muttered. "*I* don't even believe it!"

"She said she'd be back," Mother said quietly.

"She what?" shouted Daddy. "Don't tell me you really believe in all this nonsense! Why, if she comes back, I'll . . . I'll . . . I'll . . . eat my hat," he finished helplessly.

"Will you let her stay?" I asked in a small voice. "If Hilary comes back, will you let her stay?"

"She won't come back," said Daddy impatiently. "She—whoever she is—has never been here. We must have—I don't know—imagined her or something." But his voice trailed off, and even he began to look doubtful.

"But if she comes back," I persisted, "then we'll know she's really a fairy, and can she stay?"

"*If* she comes back," returned Daddy, "and this is how sure I am that she won't—*if* she comes back, she can stay. In your room."

7

"Oh, thank you, sir," said Hilary, appearing on the backseat again. "I'll be good. I promise."

Daddy just stared. Mother opened her mouth to speak, then thought better of it. I clapped my hands and let out a loud cheer.

Suddenly Daddy grinned. He reached across the front seat and put his hand out to Hilary.

"Welcome to the family, Hilary," he said. "It might be fun to have you."

"Maybe we'd better go home," said Mother. "If Hilary is staying, I have a million things to do, and it's getting late."

Hilary's face fell. "Please," she began, "oh, please . . ."

"Please what, dear?" asked Mother.

"Please can't we go to the museum? I've been waiting and waiting."

So go to the museum we did. Hilary liked the dinosaurs best. I liked the pretend cave, as usual.

2

Hilary Settles In

Hilary loved our house, especially my room. When we finally got home that evening, she ran about touching the soft eyelet curtains at the windows and admiring the wallpaper. She rubbed her cheek on the sweet-smelling towels Mother brought in for her from the linen closet. She bounced on the bed. King Arthur, our haughty tiger cat, stalked in to check her out, but stayed only a moment. He headed quickly back to the door, his fur spiking out, then turned and stared at Hilary for a long thoughtful moment from the hall.

"The bed you're on is yours," I told Hilary, going to the closet to get an extra blanket. "And the other bed is mine. And we can share the bureau and the closet—"

Suddenly I realized Hilary hadn't brought

anything to put in a closet. All she had were the clothes she was wearing.

"Do you need to borrow a nightgown?" I

asked hesitantly. "Or a toothbrush or something?"

"Not to worry." Hilary waved a hand, and at once she was wearing flowered pajamas, yellow and old fashioned, with ruffles on the front. She spun around proudly to show me.

"How did you do that?" I demanded. Hilary didn't have a magic wand, and if she'd said

any magic words, she'd said them to herself. And she didn't have wings either—at least not wings that showed under her pajamas.

A yellow toothbrush suddenly appeared on the guest bed.

"Oh, Hilary, will you show me? Can you teach me?"

Hilary shook her head.

"You won't? Why not?"

"Because then it won't be magic anymore." Hilary bent down to roll up the legs of her pajamas. When she looked up again, her eyes were round and serious. "And there's one other thing, Caroline. No one else besides the people in this house can know I'm a fairy. If anyone else finds out, I'll have to disappear."

"Do you mean disappear for *good*?" I asked her. "Or could you come back again, like you did in the car?"

"I could never come back," said Hilary. "Never. That's the rule."

I hadn't known fairies came with rules, but Hilary sounded as if she meant business. I ran downstairs to warn Mother and Daddy.

"Oh, dear," said Mother. "How will we explain her arrival then? What will we say to the school tomorrow?"

Mother thought for a moment, then decided to call Mrs. Bethany, the school principal, at home. Mother and Mrs. Bethany had gone to college together. When Mother came back to the living room after making her call, she had a big smile on her face.

"Sort of a cousin, I told her," she reported smugly. "Who's come unexpectedly to stay with us. I talked really fast, and I think she bought it."

"Honestly, Marla," Daddy said, rattling his newspaper in disapproval. "I think you're positively enjoying this. Telling stories to the principal at your age!"

"Well, I had to, didn't I?" Mother said calmly. "And you must admit this is a special case."

"Start a story and you never know where it leads," warned Daddy.

"At least Hilary doesn't have wings to give her away," I said. "Do you, Hilary? Or are they collapsible?"

"No wings," said Hilary.

"But you can fly?" I needed reassurance on this.

Hilary wiggled her hips and rose several feet above the floor. Daddy started coughing so hard Mother had to pound him on the back.

"Well, she's a fairy!" I told him when his face went back to its regular color.

"Are they all like you?" I asked Hilary curiously. "I mean, I always thought fairies were teeny and—" I almost said "beautiful" but stopped myself because I didn't want Hilary to think I didn't consider her pretty enough for a fairy. "And wore long gowns and had wings. But you just look like . . . anyone," I finished weakly.

"Well, as you said, wings would give her away," Mother pointed out. "Am I right, Hilary? So it makes sense that fairies have to look like humans when they come to visit. That way no one will know they're fairies."

Hilary nodded, and there was no arguing with Mother's logic. But could fairies take on

any human form? Boys? Old women? I started to think who of the people I knew might be a fairy in disguise—it couldn't be someone I'd known a long time, not if fairies came only for visits. Jason Markoff was new to my class, but there was no way in the world *he* was magic.

But how about Margie's great-aunt who'd come from New York last Fourth of July, or that nice new librarian? I'd have to think differently about people I met from now on.

Suddenly it seemed too much to take in all at once. And Daddy was looking pointedly at his watch, which meant it must be getting close to bedtime.

"Time to go upstairs," I told Hilary. "But I'm really glad you're here, and I promise I'll keep your secret. Though I wish I could tell just *one* friend. Maybe just Margie, or Helene. . . ."

Hilary shook her head firmly.

"Okay, I won't!" I said quickly. "And Mother won't give it away either. And Daddy . . ."

We all turned to look at my father. Daddy looked at the floor, then at the ceiling. He folded his newspaper carefully. He cleared his throat.

"You'll keep Hilary's secret too, won't you?"

"Did anyone hear me say otherwise?" he said gruffly.

3

King Arthur Goes to School

"Since it's King Arthur's birthday today," Hilary was saying, "I think we should give him a present."

"I was thinking that too," I said, not to be outdone by Hilary. After all, Arthur was my cat. "But Arthur's so picky. Whatever we give him will have to be really special." I gave my teeth a few extra bushes. "I know, Hilary," I said casually. "How about something magic?"

It wasn't every day I could get Hilary to do magic. She'd been with us for about a month now, but having a fairy around wasn't anything like I'd expected. Although Hilary was agreeable about most things, the only time I could get her to show off her magic was in the house, when she might use it to help empty the dishwasher or make the beds or collect the trash.

Try as I might—and you can be sure I tried—I never figured out how Hilary worked even that much magic. She had no magic wand, and if she said any special words, she said them to herself. When I asked Hilary about the magic, she always told me the same thing: "If I explain it, it won't be magic any more, and if it's not magic, you don't need me to explain it." That's all she would say, not one word more. So after a while, I stopped asking.

But since Hilary really liked King Arthur, I thought I could take advantage of his birthday to get her to do an extra trick or two.

"Here's an idea," I told her. "Why don't you give Arthur the power to talk for the whole day of his birthday? Then he can tell us himself how he wants to celebrate."

Hilary looked uncertain. "I guess I could," she said. "I just don't know how well magic's going to work with Arthur. Cats are really hard sometimes because they're so independent."

I snorted. Independent! Arthur thought he ruled the world.

"Please, Hilary? It would be so much fun," I begged her. "I bet Arthur would love it."

Hilary glanced at her watch. "I'm not sure we have time," she hedged.

"Sure we do. School doesn't start for another half hour. Wait here! I'll just go run and find him."

I was out the door before Hilary could change her mind. Finding Arthur in his usual morning spot by the hall radiator, I hauled him back to Hilary, but as soon as I got to the bedroom, he leaped to the floor, bristling with indignation.

"First of all," he said, "let me tell you how much I dislike being carried around."

I looked at Hilary with delight. She hadn't wasted a minute.

"And second of all," Arthur went on, "I would like you to call me King Arthur, not Arthur. I hate the name Arthur. The only good thing about being named Arthur is being King. And third of all—"

"Arthur," I interrupted. "I mean, King Arthur. Could you please stop complaining for a minute and tell me something? What do you want for your birthday?"

"I want to go to school with you and Hilary."

"Cats aren't allowed at school," I said with surprise. "If you go, they'll just send you home. Ask for something else."

"That's what I want," insisted Arthur. "Besides, they won't send me home if they don't know I'm there. All Hilary has to do is make me invisible."

"Could you do that?" I asked Hilary excitedly.

"I think so," said Hilary, studying Arthur. "I just don't know if I should."

"Come on! It's his birthday!" I pleaded. I really wanted to see this happen. "King Arthur won't give away your secret, will you, Arthur?"

"Of course I won't," said Arthur impatiently. "Once I get near the school, you won't hear a sound out of me. No one will even know I'm there. I don't want Hilary to have to disappear any more than you do."

"Hilary! Caroline!" Mother called at that moment. "Time to get a move on!"

I turned to Hilary. She looked at Arthur again and nodded.

"Okay, Arthur," I said. "You can go. Are you ready, Arthur? Where are you, Arthur?"

"Call me by my right name and I'll tell you," said a voice somewhere around my left ankle.

All morning at school, I wondered whether Arthur was enjoying himself. Most of the time, I didn't know exactly where he was, but at lunchtime he brushed up against my legs for some of my tuna sandwich. During lunch recess in the school yard, the sparrows and jays almost gave away our secret by flapping noisily up into the trees and fussing and scolding. No one could explain what was happening. Hilary and I pretended to be mystified too.

After recess we returned to our desks to work with Miss Ellison, the music teacher, on the songs from *Snow White*. We were performing the play for the lower grades in two weeks, and I was going to have the part of Snow White. Hilary was Sneezy.

It was while we were singing the dwarves' marching song that I noticed King Arthur's tail—that is, the tip of it—waving in time to the music. I was frantic. Hilary's invisible spell was wearing off, and sooner or later someone was going to notice.

I had to get her attention! But Hilary's desk was several rows in front of mine, and her eyes were fixed on Miss Ellison, who was waving a ruler in time to the music.

"Heigh-ho, heigh-ho," sang Hilary.

"Pssst!" I hissed urgently, raising myself slightly in my chair. "Hilary. Back here. I've got to tell you something."

Hilary looked over her shoulder.

"It's Arthur," I began, but Miss Ellison interrupted me. All music stopped, and the room was suddenly in silence.

"What is it, Caroline?" asked Miss Ellison. "Would you care to tell us what's so important that you can't wait to tell Hilary? We have a play to put on in two weeks, you know."

Every pair of eyes in the room was staring at me now, and my face was burning. But at least no one was looking at King Arthur's tail, which had stopped waving but was still visible in the aisle beside me. I had to do something fast, though, or Hilary wasn't going to be around to *be* in the play in two weeks.

"I . . . um . . . wanted to tell Hilary there was a problem with her . . . um . . . spelling!" I said clearly, praying Hilary would understand. "You know, Hilary, the *SPELL*-ing you did this morning?"

King Arthur understood. His tail whipped

down flat against the floor, hugging the worn gray tiles. It trembled for a moment, then lay still.

"My spelling?" said Hilary, frowning. Miss Ellison frowned too, her patience wearing thin.

I took a deep breath. "Yes, your spelling, Hilary. I just wanted you to know you need to correct it. Because if you don't, then everyone will see the mistake you made at the *TAIL* end of the lesson."

"Oh-hhh," said Hilary, turning pale. Her eyes grew wide, and I signaled with a tilt of my

head the direction of the problem. Almost immediately Arthur's tail disappeared completely. I sank back into my chair.

"Caroline, are you all right?" said Miss Ellison. "Do you need some fresh air? Do you want to lie down?"

"I'm fine, Miss Ellison," I said politely. "I was just worried about the spelling. I should have waited. Sorry."

Miss Ellison gave me one more searching look, then waved her ruler again.

"All right, class. One, two, three!"

"Heigh-ho, heigh-ho," sang King Arthur softly beside me.

Hilary and I walked home together after school, as always. King Arthur, visible now, walked beside us, striped tail high and proud and waving in time to remembered music.

"That was really close," I said to Hilary. "It's lucky I saw that spell wearing off. You sure were right about cats being tricky."

"Don't blame me," said Arthur with dignity. "Cats are what they are. And proud of it, I might add."

I grinned at Hilary. "Well, at least you got to go to school," I told Arthur. "I hope you enjoyed it."

"Indeed I did," he said. "Especially the music. In fact, I was wondering— Do you suppose there might be a part for me in *Snow*

White? I wouldn't expect to have actual lines. . . ."

"I don't think so, Arthur," I said quickly. "Though I'm sure you'd be awfully good at it."

"Indeed I would. Sometimes I think school's wasted on people. In fact," he said, tossing his head, "I know it is."

Arthur marched off down the street, humming softly. Halfway down the block he stopped and looked back.

"Remember," he called. "Ten candles on the cake. And Hilary, Caroline . . ."

"Yes, King Arthur?" I replied.

"Before it's too late . . ."

"Yes, King Arthur?" said Hilary.

"Thank you."

4

You Can Never Tell with Witches

"What are you going to be for Halloween?"

It was late October, and the children in the neighborhood talked endlessly about their costumes. Margie was going to be a fish, and Helene was going to be a bunch of grapes, and Sadie was going to be a cheerleader. Tara couldn't decide what to be. When someone suggested that Tara go as a fairy, Hilary and I had to bite our lips to keep from laughing.

Hilary had never been trick-or-treating. She thought it was a fine idea, especially the part about the candy. Hilary loved sweets. We planned our route carefully. Hilary wanted to visit as many houses as possible. I wanted to include the house on the hill.

"It's haunted," I told Hilary.

Hilary looked doubtful.

"Honest, Hilary. Maybe ghosts live there. Or witches. Everyone says so."

"Probably no one lives there," said Hilary. "We never see anyone there."

"That's because it's haunted," I explained patiently.

"Anyway," said Hilary, "we'll waste fifteen perfectly good minutes going up that long driveway."

"Well, I'm going," I told her. "If you're too scared, you can just wait at the foot of the drive."

On Halloween night, Hilary and I were in our costumes early, but we waited until dark before leaving the house. We had decided to go as witches. We smeared our hands and faces with green makeup and drew wicked eyebrows on each other with burnt cork.

Hilary sprinkled powder on her hair, and I wore a tangle of gray yarn under my pointed hat. At the last minute, I made Hilary blacken her front teeth, because she still didn't look scary enough to be a witch. The black teeth did the job so well that I decided to blacken mine too.

It was my idea to bring King Arthur with us. Hilary invited him and even managed to talk him into dressing up. Dusted with ashes from the fireplace, he looked almost black, and under cover of night, he made a very suitable witch's cat.

By the time we set forth, doorbells were ringing up and down the block. In no time, we had our bags heavy with candy. Hilary wanted to eat hers right then, but Mother and Daddy had made us promise we'd wait till we got home.

It was half past eight when we reached the long driveway that led up to the house on the hill. Our bags weighed so much by then that we had to keep switching them from one hand to the other. No one else had ventured this far down the block, and the street was dark and very quiet. We stood at the foot of the driveway and looked up at the big house, which was brightly lighted as if someone expected company. Arthur rubbed uncertainly against Hilary's ankles.

"We have to be home at nine," said Hilary hopefully.

"There's plenty of time."

"I'll wait here," said Hilary. "I'll be the guard. You ought to have a guard."

"No way," I said and, grabbing Hilary's hand, pulled her after me up the driveway.

The drive was clear, but the path to the house was badly overgrown, and we had to go single file. I went first; Hilary and Arthur trailed a short distance behind. The front steps were almost hidden. I was beginning to wish I hadn't insisted on coming, when the front door creaked open, even before we rang.

Hilary gasped. There before us, black against a rectangle of light, was the figure of a witch.

The figure moved. Hilary gasped again.

The witch was dressed much as we were, in a long black robe and a tall pointed hat, but she was much larger than we were and far more frightening. Her nose reached almost to her chin, her eyes were smudged with purple, and her fingernails were horribly long and curved and painted black.

"Come in, come in," she said pleasantly enough. "Have you come for the meeting?"

"What meeting?" I whispered as the door closed behind us.

"Why, the annual meeting of witches," she said, looking at us in a puzzled way. "It's Halloween, you know."

"No, I mean, yes," I stammered. "I mean— do you live here?"

"Yes, I do," she replied. "And where do you live? I thought all the local witches were relatives of mine, but I haven't seen you two before. Are you out-of-town witches?"

She smiled at us, but we didn't smile back.

She looked at our solemn faces and shook her head slightly.

"Oh, dear," she murmured to herself. "I wonder if . . ." She reached down and put a long finger under Hilary's chin, then under mine.

"Please," I said hoarsely. "Please—trick or treat?"

The big witch turned and walked off down the long hall. Hilary and I looked at each other.

"What if she's really a witch?" I whispered. "We'd better get out of here."

"Maybe she just went to get candy," protested Hilary.

"It could be a trap," I said. "Witches do that, you know. Pretend to be nice, and then . . . !"

Hilary looked doubtful.

"You can never tell with witches, Hilary!"

"Girls," sang out the witch from somewhere at the other end of the house. "I'll be there in a minute."

I tugged at Hilary's arm.

"She'll come after us!" I said urgently. "Come on, Hilary, can't you put a spell on her or something?"

"I know what I'll do," said Hilary. "I'll call for help. There are lots of fairies in the neighborhood tonight. I saw them on the way up."

At first I didn't believe her.

"Other fairies? Real fairies?"

Then I remembered. Mr. Mellon had told us just the other day in school that people used to believe that fairies traveled about on All Hallow's Eve. Fairies—and witches!

"Will the fairies come, Hilary? Will you call them?"

"I already have," said Hilary, smiling. "Listen!"

The doorbell rang and rang again. The chimes rang out merrily in the big old hall, and we could hear the sound of voices and laughter on the other side of the witch's great front door. Arthur made a funny sound deep in his throat, and the fur on his back stood suddenly on end.

Hilary winked at me and reached to open the door. A crowd of figures spilled forth into the hall. These were no ordinary trick-or-treaters. A queen in royal purple, with a jeweled crown on her head, came smiling and waving, her long train held by two velvety gray mice. Then a clown in red silk somersaulted in, followed by Captain Hook and Raggedy Ann and a gingerbread man who smelled good enough to eat. A floppy pink elephant was next, with a ballerina on his back. They kept coming until they filled the room. There was even a fairy (as I had always imagined fairies, before Hilary) wearing a gown that looked like moonlight, with transparent wings that fluttered as she danced and twirled about.

"Welcome! Welcome!" said the witch, hurrying down the hall with a basket of candy.

"Trick or treat!" cried the newcomers. "Trick or treat!"

We all held out our bags, and the witch chattered as she dropped a generous handful of sweets in each one.

"I'm so glad you've come," she kept saying. "Usually nobody comes, way up here on the hill, you know. Except," she said, smiling at Hilary and me, "for a few witches, from time to time. But I've always been ready. Every year."

"Here, take another piece," she said to Hilary. "And someone take a handful for the elephant."

The pink elephant bowed his thanks. Then he turned slightly and did a little shuffling dance step. Raggedy Ann caught hold of his tail and stretched her hand out to the fairy. Hilary pushed me into line after the fairy, and the clown came prancing after me. Soon we were all part of a dancing, laughing chain—even Arthur, whom Hilary scooped up and set precariously on the elephant's back. We formed a circle and danced three times around the hall, trick-or-treat bags swinging from our arms. The witch, in the center of the circle, clapped her hands in time to our footsteps. She no longer seemed frightening at all.

Three times around. Then the elephant, again taking the lead, broke the circle and, stretching out his trunk, opened the witch's front door. Out he danced into the night, the rest of us close behind him.

"Good night!" I called to the witch, who stood in the doorway waving happily to us all. "Happy Halloween!"

Still smiling, the witch pulled the big door shut. Without the light from the house, it was suddenly very dark outside. And very quiet. I looked around.

"Where are they all?"

I could have cried with disappointment.

"Where have they all gone?"

Of all the merrymakers, only Hilary and I and Arthur remained.

"Couldn't they have stayed?" I asked Hilary sadly.

Hilary shook her head. "Time to go," she said briskly. "It's almost nine. Hurry, Caroline."

I didn't say a word all the way home. I was too busy remembering.

"Hilary," I said finally as we were walking up the front porch steps. "Do you think she was really a witch?"

"I don't know," said Hilary. "What do you think?"

"I hope so," I answered. "Now that it's over. How about you, Arthur? Do you think that woman was a witch?"

"Rrrow," said Arthur. He settled on his haunches by the front door and began to lick the fireplace dust carefully from his shoulders.

5

The Tallest Snowman

I made my way down to the bottom of the bed and pulled back the curtains.

"Whoopee!" I yelled. "There's tons of it! Wake up, Hilary! There's snow outside!"

I rushed through breakfast and stamped impatiently in the back hall while Hilary tied her hood and adjusted the fasteners on her shiny rubber boots. Finally she was ready. I bounded down the back steps and landed joyfully in a huge snowdrift. Hilary stepped more carefully.

"What do we do now?" Hilary asked.

"Let's make a snowman," I suggested.

"How do you make a snowman?"

I couldn't believe it. She'd never made a snowman!

I showed Hilary how to roll a ball in the snow until it was big and round. It was slow work because the snow was quite deep and wet, and it was hard to move the balls around the yard. King Arthur, who hated snow, picked his way across our tracks and hopped up into a cleared patch on top of the picnic table to watch us work.

It took Hilary and me about half an hour to get three large balls made and stacked on top of one another.

"Now we have to find stones and things to make him a face," I said. "I just wish he could be taller, though."

"Why can't he?"

"We can't reach any higher," I pointed out. "We almost couldn't get the third ball on top." Suddenly I had an idea. "Unless you could fly it up," I said hopefully.

Hilary didn't reply.

"With all this good deep snow, we could make a zillion balls, Hilary. We could make the tallest snowman in the world!"

Hilary looked around the yard. She knew how much I loved seeing her magic.

"There aren't any neighbors out," I told her. "And we're so far back from the street no one can see us."

"Okay," Hilary relented. "Let's get going."

As soon as we'd finished our next snowball, Hilary squatted down to put her arms around it. The ball was almost as big as she was. Heaving it up off the ground, she looked carefully around her, wiggled her hips a bit, and flew up to place the snowball on top of the other three. King Arthur raised his head and sat still as a statue, watching Hilary drift back to earth.

I too was transfixed. Of all Hilary's magic, her flying was what I envied most. I wiggled my hips as she had. I flapped my arms. Of course, nothing happened.

"Come on," Hilary said, dragging me over

to the snowiest part of the yard. "Let's make more."

While we were working, I tried to convince Hilary to let me fly the next snowball up.

"I can't," she told me.

"Can't what?" I asked her. "Can't let me put the snowball on, or can't make me fly?"

"Just 'can't,'" she told me.

"Why not? Tinkerbell made Wendy fly in *Peter Pan*."

"That was *Peter Pan*," said Hilary, pushing the snowball she was working on in the other direction. She reminded me of King Arthur, who always showed his displeasure by sitting down, turning his back on us, and thumping his tail on the floor.

"Okay, okay, you can do the flying," I called to her. "But let's at least try and use up all the snow in the yard!"

As the afternoon wore on, Hilary flew up snowball after snowball. Finally the snowman got so wobbly that even I was afraid to make him taller, and Hilary went inside to ask Mother for a carrot and our old top hat. I volunteered to dig under the snow at the foot of the driveway for stones.

"I found two stones exactly alike for the eyes," I told Hilary when she came back out again, "and this pile of little ones can go all in a row for the mouth." I gave Hilary the stones and looked carefully around.

"No one's looking," I said. "Except Arthur."

Hilary flew up and began to arrange the snowman's face.

"Make him smile," I said. "Put the end stones of his mouth up a bit."

When Hilary had placed the top hat on the

snowman's head, she flew back a few feet to look at her creation.

"Terrific," I said. "But he needs a broom. I saw an old one out near the street. I'll be back in a minute."

Struggling to get the broom out of a snowdrift, I heard someone come up behind me.

"What's that for?" Corky Herman asked. Corky, who was a grade ahead of me, was with his buddy Brian, and I detested both of them. Ordinarily I'd have just walked off, but I was so excited I couldn't resist bragging about the snowman.

"Wait till you see," I told them. "Hilary and I made a snowman, and you won't believe how big he is. This broom's for him," I added, wrenching the broom from the snowdrift.

"Who cares?" Corky said. "I once made a snowman that was six feet high. Seven feet!"

"Ours is bigger," I told him.

Corky and Brian followed when I went back up the drive. "Hil-a-ry!" I yelled anxiously. "Company coming!"

"What's so great about a tall snowman?" said Brian. "Right, Corky?"

"Right," agreed Corky. Then he caught sight of it.

"You didn't make that," he said to me accusingly. "And neither did Hilary. She's not even as big as you are."

"We did so make him," I retorted. "Didn't we, Hilary?"

Hilary nodded.

"Then somebody helped you. A grown-up."

"Nope. No grown-ups. I swear."

"Then how did you do it?"

"Magic," I said blithely. Maybe I shouldn't have taken the chance, but I knew Corky would never take me seriously.

Hilary stared at me, aghast.

"Oh, cut it out," said Corky. "Did you use a ladder?"

"Nope," I said. "No ladder."

"Did you stand on a pile of snow?"

"Nope," I said, grinning. "Magic."

Hilary grabbed me. "Caroline!"

"These two are weirdos, you know that, Bri?" said Corky. "Maybe they *did* do something weird."

Hilary's fingers dug into my arm, and I had a terrible feeling I might have taken my joke too far. But then Brian's face lit up suddenly.

"A helicopter!" he shouted. "I bet they lowered the stuff from a helicopter."

I could almost feel Hilary's knees wobbling along with my own. "That's goofy," I told him giddily. "Where'd we get a helicopter?"

"You're goofy," retorted Corky. "How'd you do it? And don't say magic this time. There's no such thing as magic. Right, Bri?" He gave Brian a nudge with his elbow.

I shrugged and turned my back on him, propping the old broom against the snowman. "Do you think he needs arms, Hilary?" I said.

"We'll help," said Corky slyly. "Show us how."

Did Corky really believe I was going to fall for that? "You'd never reach," I said, shaking my head.

"Who cares about the dumb snowman?" muttered Corky. "I bet it wouldn't take much to knock it over anyway."

That should have warned me. Corky and Brian were halfway down the driveway when suddenly they turned and marched slowly and deliberately back toward the snowman.

"Hilary!" I whispered. "Do something! They're going to wreck him—I know it!"

"What do you want me to do?" she whispered back.

How was I supposed to know? Corky and Brian were grinning nastily. Too late I wished we'd built a fort around the snowman— maybe then we could have defended him. Or built him against the garage so he couldn't topple.

Brian stumbled. Go ahead, fall, Brian, I said to myself. I hope you slide all the way down the driveway!

I clapped my snow-encrusted mitten over my mouth. "That's it, Hilary," I whispered behind it. "Make it slippery. Around the snowman. With your magic. NOW!"

I charged the boys and tried to block them to give Hilary time, but all I managed to do was grab Brian's jacket and pull him around.

When Corky tried to free him, I heard something rip and automatically loosened my fingers. I could just hear what my mother would say if I tore someone's jacket.

"Watch out. Here they come!" I yelled to Hilary as Corky and Brian rushed the snowman.

"What can *I* do?" she shouted. But something about her voice got my attention. In a large circle around the snowman, where our snowball-making had worn away the snow down to the grass, there was now a solid sheet of ice. Red-faced and panting, the boys struggled to get to the snowman but kept sliding backward, their target always six inches from their grasp. Over and over they tried, feet churning uselessly, until finally Corky made a

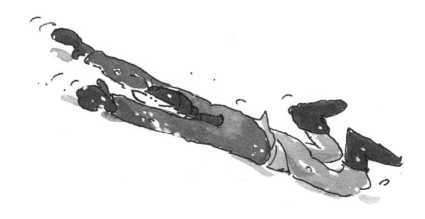

desperate attempt to fling himself across the ice, and his feet went out from under him. Landing with a loud "ooomph" on his stomach, he slid slowly down the slope toward the drive.

Stoney-faced, he got up and slapped snow from his jacket. He threw one last baleful look back at the snowman. "Let's go, Bri," he growled, and the two headed down the driveway.

But Corky had one final surprise for us. Pulling a large, hard-packed snowball from his jacket pocket, he turned quickly, narrowed his eyes, and hurled the ball deliberately at the snowman's head.

"Oh, no!" I wailed. The ball was traveling straight and sure, with enough force to topple the already precarious snowman.

Hilary smiled. For an instant, Corky's snowball seemed to stop in midair, where it hovered for a moment, glittering in the afternoon sun. Then as we all watched openmouthed, it fell apart harmlessly in a silent shower of tiny snowflakes.

"Too bad, Corky!" I shouted. Hilary elbowed me into silence.

Corky shrugged and kept walking, Brian a few steps behind. Hilary and I stood without moving.

At the end of the drive, Corky hesitated for a moment. Then he shoved his mittened

hands deep into his jacket pockets and headed off down the street.

"There's no such thing as magic!" he yelled back over his shoulder.

"That shows how much you know," said the snowman quietly. King Arthur's head came up with a jerk. Hilary and I burst out laughing. The snowman winked at us, his smile wider than ever.

6

The Magic Magic Show

"Susie's having a magician at her party," I told Hilary as we walked up the front steps to Susie's house. "I just love magicians, don't you?"

"I don't know," said Hilary. "I've never seen one. Do they really do magic?"

"Well, sort of. Their kind of magic, anyway."

"Maybe I'll learn some new tricks," said Hilary.

Just then, before I could ask if Hilary was joking, Tara and Louise came up behind us.

"Hi, guys," I said. "I didn't know you'd be here."

"I wouldn't miss this party for anything," said Tara. "Did you know? There's going to be a magician!"

Ten of us were seated in a semicircle on Susie's living-room floor when Alfonso the Magnificent swept into the room with a flourish and bowed deeply before us. Most of us were used to having family members perform magic tricks at birthday parties, but Alfonso was a professional, a real magician.

"La-dies and gentlemen!" he began.

"There aren't any gentlemen," my friends Helene and Margie called out in unison.

"Then . . . ladies and ladies," returned Alfonso. We all giggled. "I am de-lighted to be here at Susie's birthday party. I have brought the birthday girl a white rose—" he gave Susie the rose he was holding "—and I have for each of her guests a similar rose of red. Here in my hat."

Alfonso held out his tall black hat for us to

look at. There was nothing in it but a maroon
silk lining.

"Now who would like a rose?" With a lightning move of his gloved hand, Alfonso
reached into the hat. He searched inside,
then searched some more. Then he turned
his back to us, the folds of his cape swirling
around him. He appeared to be shaking the
hat. And shaking it again.

"Alas, ladies and ladies," he said finally. "It
seems that red roses are out of season. I shall
mail one to each of you in the summer. In the
meantime . . . what do you hear?"

We listened. I thought I heard a puppy bark.

"Yes, ladies and ladies, it is a puppy," said Alfonso. "You hear it, but do you see it? Does anyone see it?"

"I bet it's in your box," said Gina, pointing to the large black suitcase on the floor behind Alfonso.

"It's not in my box," said Alfonso smoothly. "It's nowhere. But soon it will be somewhere, and then it will be elsewhere. Watch me carefully."

Alfonso took a red silk scarf from his pocket and shook it before us. "You see the scarf," he said. "Nothing is in it, nothing is on it, nothing is under it. Now watch!"

The puppy barked again. Alfonso passed the scarf over his right hand. He made the pass again. And again.

"What's happening?" I whispered to Hilary.

"I have a terrible feeling," she whispered back, "that it's all my fault. Maybe I'd better leave."

Hilary looked worried.

"It's my magic," she explained, leaning closer so she could keep her voice down. "My magic is so much stronger than his that his won't work."

"But you can't leave!" I said. "What will we tell everyone?"

"Watch again," Alfonso was saying. His face was getting purple. Someone snickered.

"Hilary," I whispered. "Is there some way you could help him? With *your* magic? I mean, some way that nobody would notice?"

"How?" said Hilary.

"I don't know. Maybe you could do the magic and make it seem like his. No one will get suspicious if a *magician's* doing magic. It's probably safer than explaining why we're leaving."

"What are you two talking about?" Margie asked curiously. "Did you say something about leaving, Caroline?"

"Shhh-hh, everyone!" said Susie. "Watch what Alfonso's doing. He's trying again."

Once more the magician passed the scarf over his hand. But this time when he whipped the scarf off, there was a fuzzy yellow puppy sitting in his hand.

"Voila!" Alfonso said with relief. "Stubborn little thing, aren't you?"

"Look on your shoulder!" squealed Gina.

Alfonso's eyes grew wide. A second puppy, this one a brown one, was sitting on his shoulder. "Er—hello," said Alfonso. Then suddenly he shook his left leg. An all-black puppy scampered out from under the cuff of his pants.

Everyone—everyone but me, that is— applauded wildly. Alfonso looked dazed. I wasn't at all sure I liked the way this situation was developing. My idea had just been for Hilary to help Alfonso do his own magic, not to fancy it up with her own.

"And now for my next trick . . . ," Alfonso was announcing weakly. "My next trick is . . . at least I think it is . . ."

"Hilary!" I whispered, but she was watching Alfonso so intently I couldn't get her attention. He turned and took from his black case a wooden box and a doll, then automatically opened the wooden box so we could see it was empty. He passed the doll around so we could examine it. But all the time, he was looking at the two extra puppies and shaking his head.

I tried once more. "Hilary!"

Susie glared at me.

"Now, er—ladies and ladies," said Alfonso. "I shall put this perfectly ordinary doll in this perfectly ordinary box and close the lid. I shall then take my sword from this sheath at my side—and—cut the box in two. Miss Susie, will you be so kind as to examine the box for me to make sure that it's in two separate pieces?"

Susie jumped up and ran her hand over the surface of the two boxes. All around.

"Now if you will remain and watch me," said the magician to Susie, "I shall fit the two pieces back together—so!—and remove the lid. You see?" Alfonso breathed a sigh of relief. "It is the doll—still in one piece!"

We all clapped. So did the doll. When Alfonso saw what was happening, he jumped back and let go of the doll so fast she tumbled to the floor. But that wasn't the end of it. The doll got up, brushed herself off, did a few dance steps, then hopped back into the box and lay down, as still as she had been before.

Hilary grinned slightly.

"Wow," said Helene to no one in particularly. "He's good, isn't he?"

"I want to see the doll," called Gina.

"I want to hold the puppies," said Adrienne. "I haven't had a turn yet." She looked around the room. "Hey, where are the other two puppies?"

Suddenly there was confusion. All of us got up and ran about Susie's house looking for the puppies. I tried to get Hilary off in a corner to warn her about getting too far ahead of Alfonso with her magic, but Helene came after us and we had to cut off the conversation. Finally Susie's mother herded us all back to the living room.

"Alfonso says," she told us firmly, "that the show must go on. Isn't that right, Mr. Alfonso?"

"But what happened to the other two puppies?" insisted Adrienne. "It's *my* turn!"

"The puppies," said Susie's mother, "are magician's puppies. You have to expect them to disappear, right, Mr. Alfonso?"

"I guess so," said Alfonso, wiping his forehead with his red scarf. "If you say so."

Adrienne persisted. "But where did they—"

"Alfonso said the show must go ON," Susie bellowed, much to my relief, and she pushed the original yellow puppy at Adrienne, who finally sat down grumbling. Alfonso gave himself a little shake and returned to business.

"I think we have time for one last trick," he said. "For this trick, I need a helper. How about you, Miss, in the blue dress?"

I glanced at Hilary with alarm and rose slowly.

"That's Caroline," shouted Margie.

"Ah, Miss Caroline," said Alfonso. "May I please explain what I want you to do? I shall sit in this desk chair—so!—and you will take this rope and tie me to it. Hands and legs, please, and do your very best job of tying."

Since I didn't know what Hilary's plans were, I just followed Mr. Alfonso's instructions. I wound the rope in an intricate pattern around his arms and legs, hoping I wasn't making things too hard for Hilary.

"Good job," Gina told me approvingly as I went back to my place. "Okay, Alfonso, what are you going to do now?"

Alfonso's eyes widened. He wiggled his arms. Then he wiggled his legs. Then he wiggled the chair. Nothing happened, except that his face got red again. I prayed Hilary knew what she was doing.

"Abracadabra!" said Alfonso suddenly. He looked startled. "Did I say that?" he said. Then he gave his right hand an impatient wiggle and all at once he was holding a huge bunch of bright balloons, each a different glorious color. He opened his hand quickly and the balloons sailed to the ceiling and disappeared.

Alfonso wiggled his left hand. A white dove appeared and perched on his open palm. She spread her wings, flew three times around the living room, then vanished out an open window.

"My word," murmured Susie's mother.

Alfonso looked curiously at his right foot. He gave it a wiggle. His shiny black shoe turned red, then purple, then gold, then orange, then green-and-silver-striped, then back to shiny black again.

"Ooooh!" said Gina. No one else said a word.

Alfonso wiggled his left foot. A cloud of blue smoke rose from the floor and hid the magician from sight. When the smoke cleared, I clapped until my hands hurt. Alfonso's rope had been turned into a shiny scarlet ribbon, tied at the very top of his head in an enormous scarlet bow. Alfonso the Magnificent looked like a rather silly, very embarrassed birthday present!

"Miss Caroline?" whispered Hilary in the tiniest of voices.

Somehow this time I knew exactly what to do. I rose again, took hold of one end of the scarlet bow, and pulled it gently. The ribbons fell away from Alfonso's arms and legs, and the magician rose to receive his applause.

And how everyone applauded!

"It was a super show," I told Hilary proudly on the way home. "The best magic show ever. And I don't think anyone suspected a thing, do you?"

Hilary shook her head. "Except maybe poor Mr. Alfonso."

"Well, *he* won't tell anyone—he got all the

credit even though you did all the work! He's going to be pretty surprised, though, when he tries to do it again. Anyway, I think you should do your own show sometime, Hilary— wouldn't that be neat? We could call you Hilary the Fantastic, and I could be your assistant, and we could say we'd practiced lots and that's why we were so good at it."

Hilary looked at me, and I knew what she was thinking—that it would be too risky. But still . . .

"Didn't you even care that they were clapping for him and not for you?" I demanded. I knew I'd have hated it if I'd been in her place. But Hilary just shrugged in her matter-of-fact way; I guessed maybe being able to do magic didn't seem as wonderful to her as it did to me.

Late that night, though, when we were supposed to be sleeping, I heard Hilary climb quietly out of bed. When she didn't return, I went to look for her. I found her standing in front of the big mirror in the bathroom, her yellow corduroy robe slung over her shoulders like a cape. She bowed deeply to her image in the mirror.

"La-dies and ladies!" she murmured, too engrossed to see me behind her.

I went back to our room, and a short time later, Hilary returned too.

"Good night, Miss Caroline," she whispered as she slipped into bed.

"Good night, Hilary the Fantastic," I said, grinning into the darkness. Then I burrowed under the covers and drifted off to sleep.

7

The Best Medicine

As the big jet lifted off, Hilary clutched at my arm.

"This is scary," she whispered.

"Don't worry. I've flown lots of times," I comforted her. "It's fun."

"So have I flown lots of times," returned Hilary. "But I don't ever go up this high when I fly by myself."

Hilary and I and my parents were on our way to Washington, D.C. for spring vacation. I was especially excited because we were going to be there in time for the cherry blossoms, and Mother had promised me it was a sight I'd never forget.

Soon the pilot turned off the seat-belts sign, and the flight attendants began serving drinks. I'd already picked out my favorite attendant. Her name was Sally, and she had beautiful black braids and a radiant smile. But Sally's flight wasn't going smoothly. All around me, passengers were buzzing her with special requests. The elderly woman in the red pantsuit needed help cleaning up some ginger ale she'd spilled. The businessman with the briefcase demanded immediate information about connecting flights and then shouted at Sally because he didn't like his connections. The big man with the grizzled beard wanted to change to an aisle seat, and the young father a few rows behind me needed baby bottles warmed right away for his wailing twins. Sally's smile was fading fast.

"Why are they all so crabby?" I asked Hilary indignantly. "I think she's wonderful."

"Me, too," said Hilary loyally. "Maybe they all left their smiles on the ground."

"Mother would say we need more than smiles on this plane," I observed. "This calls for giggles. Do you have any giggles, Hilary?"

"Sure." Hilary giggled.

"Enough for everyone?" I asked.

"What do you mean?" Hilary's eyes grew wide. "Oh, no, Caroline! Not here."

"Why not?" I looked around. "It would help Sally, and it would probably do everyone a lot of good. Mother always says a good giggle is the best medicine, don't you, Mother?" I asked my mother, who sat reading in the seat across the aisle.

"What, dear?" said Mother vaguely. She hadn't heard a thing. She never did when she was absorbed in her reading.

"Be good now, girls," she murmured, going back to her book.

"See, Hilary?" I said. "Not even Mother has a laugh for us. And it's vacation! People are supposed to have a good time on vacation. Do these people look like they're having a good time?"

Just then Sally tripped over the bearded man's foot and cracked her knee on the drink cart.

"I don't even know if my magic would work way up here," protested Hilary.

"Try it," I urged her. "What's the worst that could happen?"

Across the aisle Mother snickered, then snorted.

"Is your book funny?" I could hear Daddy asking as she burst into laughter. "I didn't think that was supposed to be a funny book."

"It's not." Mother threw her arms around him. "I just felt happy all of a sudden."

Daddy laughed too.

"Now this is what I call a vacation!" he said.

Delighted, I got up on my knees to see what might happen next.

"Stewardess," called the man in the striped suit who'd complained earlier about the air conditioning. "Have you heard the joke about the man in the striped suit?" He slapped his leg and began to rock with laughter. Several people around him began to laugh too.

"Oh, no," exclaimed the twins' father as one of his children sent his ball rolling merrily down the aisle.

"Catch!" said the businessman, throwing the ball back to him.

"Monkey in the middle!" shouted the woman in the red pantsuit, intercepting the ball from her aisle seat. All three began to laugh. Even the twins stopped crying.

Soon the plane was filled with a symphony of high-pitched squeaks, throaty chuckles, and shouts of delight. Sally, her smile back, started the passengers on a round of songs. Hilary and I sang louder than anybody.

The pilot decided to join the party.

"Ladies and gentlemen," boomed the loudspeaker. "Welcome aboard Flight 402, your ship of the air, where the trip is shorter, smoother, sillier, and Sallier than on any other airline. We are flying east, according to

plan, but we can go anywhere under the sun. Get it, ladies and gentlemen? Anywhere under the sun?"

"Oh, no," I groaned. "His jokes are just like my Uncle Robert's."

"Where shall we go, ladies and gentlemen?" The pilot was having a fine time now. "The sky's the limit. Get it? The sky's the limit! Shall we go to Chattanooga?"

"No-o-o!" shouted the passengers.

"Shall we go to Albuquerque?"

"No-o-o!" shouted the passengers.

"Kalamazoo?"

"Yes," yelled the man in the striped suit.

"No-o-o!" shouted everyone else.

"This is fun, isn't it?" Hilary whispered beside me.

I nodded. It didn't even seem that much like magic, except I'd never really seen grown-ups acting this silly.

"Uh-oh," said Hilary. "What's that?"

I turned quickly and buckled my seat belt. The plane was making dramatic loops in the air, weaving and turning and doubling back until I could no longer tell in which direction we were going.

I leaned across the aisle to ask Mother if she knew what was going on.

"It's to be a surprise!" said Mother, her eyes sparkling with excitement. "Weren't you just listening? The pilot was taking requests, but we couldn't agree on where to go, so he said he'd decide for us all. Where do you and Hilary hope he's going? Daddy and I are hoping for Paris."

"I don't hope anything!" I wailed. "I don't want to go somewhere else. I want to see the cherry blossoms!"

I turned to Hilary. "Oh, Hilary, it's terrible. Did you hear that? Do something, can't you?"

"What shall I do?" asked Hilary. "My magic's never turned an airplane around before. I don't even think it knows the way to Washington."

"Well, at least turn the giggles off," I pleaded. "Can you do that? If everyone stops having such a good time, maybe they'll act grown-up again and go where they're supposed to go. Hurry, Hilary—we don't want to go too much out of our way."

As usual when Hilary did her magic, I kept a careful eye on her to see how she did it. But as usual she gave nothing away.

"Stewardess!" yelled the lady in the red pantsuit.

Behind me, the twins began wailing.

"Poor Sally," I said as things got back to normal. "At least we tried."

Then I realized I still didn't know which way we were going.

"What if he's going west?" I worried. "We'll have to go all the way around the globe and back again, and that will take ages! The cherry blossoms will all be *dead* when we get to Washington!"

Then suddenly I heard something that made my cherry-blossom worries seem small. Behind us a man and a woman were discussing the pilot's fancy flying.

"Well, I think someone should know about it!" the woman said indignantly. "Loops in the air indeed! If you're not going to report it, I will!"

"I think you're right," said the man. "It's fortunate we're headed for Washington. I'll make the call right now."

I could feel our seats jiggle, and I knew they were taking the phone from its little compartment on Hilary's seat back. I considered phones on airplanes a pretty neat invention, but I was sorry now that this plane had them. I could hear the man punching in numbers and then talking, murmuring things about "irresponsible" and "investigation," and I knew Hilary could hear him too.

"What are we going to do?" I asked her.

Hilary, sitting stiff and straight in her seat, just shook her head. I had no idea if investigators could uncover magic, but I was aware they asked a lot of questions. And while they might not bother with me and Hilary, Mother and Daddy were another story entirely. Even though my parents didn't know what we'd done, they might be smart enough to guess, and if government officials started asking Daddy questions, I just knew he'd consider it his duty to answer them.

Behind us the man hung up the phone.

"Everything all right, girls?" asked Daddy from his seat across the aisle. "It won't be much longer. I can feel the plane slowing down, right on schedule."

"Everything's fine," I told him automatically, though I didn't see how things could be much worse.

As the plane came in for its landing, I got more and more anxious about what we were about to face. Would the investigators meet the plane? Would they question us on the spot? If Daddy spilled the beans, would Hilary vanish into thin air right in front of us?

I clutched Hilary's jacket sleeve as if my doing so could keep her from disappearing. Then, as we waited to get off the plane, I saw two stern men in navy blue jackets come through the door and begin talking to the pilot. I knew investigators when I saw them! The pilot's face turned gray, and I was afraid even to look at Hilary; if she had to leave us now, it would be all my fault.

There was only one thing I could think of to do. It had worked once, so why not a second time? Hilary didn't even put up her usual fuss when I whispered my plan to her. I think she was grateful I'd come up with any plan at all.

As always Hilary worked fast. Suddenly the investigators burst out laughing, great gusty shouts that rocketed around the plane. The startled pilot began chuckling also, and in seconds he too was doubled over and stamping on the floor. Their glee was contagious: before long tears were rolling down the businessman's cheeks and the lady in the red pantsuit had laughed herself into a case of the hiccups. By the time we got to the door, the pilot and the investigators, arms around one another's shoulders, had collapsed hysterically against the walls, and it was quite clear the investigation was over.

The Best Medicine

"Great flight!" called out the man in the striped suit. "I've never had such a good time!"

"If you've got to fly with little ones," yelled the twins' father, "this is the way to go."

"Write that down," gasped the younger of the two investigators between laughs. "Because we're going to see this fine crew gets a promotion!"

I don't think I'd ever been so glad to get off an airplane. Once in the airport, my knees felt like pudding; I sank onto a chair with the excuse that I had to rearrange my backpack. Hilary collapsed into the seat beside me.

"Wasn't that the wildest flight?" said Daddy, standing over us, his face still pink and smiling. "I don't know what got into everyone, but I feel fabulous!"

"Of course you do," Mother said fondly. "So do I. And no wonder! What do I always say is the best medicine?"

Hilary and I poked each other and burst out laughing.

8

Mother's Garden

The close call with the investigators really scared Hilary. For a long time, she did no magic outside the house, and that was fine with me—I'd been pretty scared too. School wound down, and summer vacation began, and we had lots to keep us busy. And then it was time for Mother's garden show.

Mother was a very nice, gentle, sensible woman about everything but her flowers. From the start of the growing season, she was outdoors every chance she got, digging and

hoeing and staking and clipping and plucking. When she really got working, she'd lose track of time, and we'd have to remind her to come in for dinner.

Most of the time, Mother enjoyed her garden, but things got tense every year just before the show. Club rules said no one but the gardener could work on the flowers for seven days before the judging, and Mother seemed to spend that whole week worrying. She worried about bugs and she worried about sun; she worried about rabbits and she worried about rain. She worried about things that had nothing to do with the show.

"You always tell me not to worry about things that can't be helped," I reminded Mother.

"I'm not worried!" retorted Mother. "Go find Hilary and play."

Late on the Saturday afternoon before the show, Mother came indoors to stay. "All finished," she announced. "There's nothing more I can do."

Hilary looked at her a little warily. She had never before had to live with Mother at garden show time.

"Maybe Hilary could do a magic spell to keep the dogs out of the garden," I suggested to Mother. "Or is that against the rules?"

Mother ruffled my hair. "I doubt if that one made the rule book," she said. "But thanks for the thought. I think everything will be fine, though. Even the weatherman's cooperating. There's only a slight possibility of thunderstorms."

But that night a storm blew up, and thunder crashed around the house. The lightning seemed unusually near, and Hilary climbed onto the foot of my bed for comfort.

"Are you afraid?" I asked wonderingly. "I wouldn't think *you'd* be afraid."

"I hardly used to notice storms at all," said Hilary. "It's different when you've been living in a house awhile."

"I'm not afraid," I said. "I like it. I wish I could go outside and dance around on the lawn."

"Just don't step on your mom's flowers," said Hilary, and we both laughed.

When we came downstairs the next morning, King Arthur was alone in the kitchen, thumping his long tail in annoyance at having to wait for breakfast. We found Mother out in the side yard, and I knew by looking at her that something was wrong. A large branch from the old hackberry tree had blown down in the storm and fallen directly across the garden.

"It's no use, girls," Mother said sadly. "There's too much damage. Some of these plants are beyond fixing, and the others— well, it's too much work to do in one morning."

"Try, Mom," I urged. "At least try. Hilary and I will get breakfast."

Hilary and I and King Arthur tiptoed around the yard most of the morning while Mother worked in the garden. Daddy finally took pity on us and invited Hilary and me out to lunch.

"Cheer up, girls," he said. "Your mother's tough. She'll give those flowers a good scolding and make 'em stand up straight."

"She'll tell them she'll take away their allowance," I joked. Daddy was trying so hard I thought I ought to try too.

Hilary didn't say a thing.

When we returned home, we could hear Mother on the phone. "I know, Mrs. Elgin," she was saying, "but the branch tore up so much I really don't have any choice but to withdraw from the judging. Yes, I'm sorry too. Maybe next year. Good-bye now."

Mother hung up and smiled at us. The kitchen table was covered with jars and vases filled with bright cut flowers. "Well, gang," she said, "the garden's moved in here."

"That bad?" asked Daddy.

"That bad," said Mother briskly. "I cut what I could to bring indoors. The garden looks as if it's had a bad haircut."

"Oh, Mother," I said sadly.

Shortly after three o'clock, the front door-bell rang. Hilary and I raced to answer it.

"I'm Mrs. Elgin," said the tall, bony lady at the door. "Is your mother home by any chance?"

Mother had followed us to the door.

"I hope you'll forgive my ringing," said Mrs. Elgin. "But I was walking by on my judging route, and I wondered if you wanted to change your mind. Why, my dear, your garden is lovely. Simply enchanting!"

"It is?" said Mother. "No, it isn't. It couldn't · be."

We all trailed Mother out to look at the garden. But it wasn't Mother's garden any more. Mother's flowers always stood at attention, row upon row of perfectly tended plants. This was a fairyland. Flowers of every variety and color were tumbled against one another, and their beauty made us catch our breath.

"However did you do it?" Mrs. Elgin asked Mother. "It's most unusual."

"I'm afraid I can't take credit for it," said Mother. She pulled Hilary and me to her and hugged us. "I had help, you see. And I know that's against the contest rules."

I certainly hadn't helped, as I told Mother after Mrs. Elgin left. I'd only wished I could.

"You helped," said Mother. "Just knowing you were on my side helped more than I can say. But the flowers—that was you, Hilary, wasn't it?"

I looked at Hilary with surprise. Was the garden magic? I knew Hilary hadn't been out gardening because I'd been with her every minute since we'd gotten up that morning, but it wasn't like Hilary to do magic on her own. She must really love Mother a lot, I decided, to have taken such a risk for her, to have put her magic out in the neighborhood where everyone could see.

"I was afraid you wouldn't like it," said

Hilary. "It's a bit untidy. But I wanted to do something—and this was the only kind of garden I knew how to do."

"It's beautiful, Hilary," said Mother. "It's the best garden I've ever had. I hope it stays like this forever."

If only Hilary had asked me first! Living with my mother, I knew gardeners, and I was sure this particular magic was going to drive

the other gardeners on the block crazy. And I
was afraid that was going to mean trouble for
Hilary.

I was right too. In less than an hour, Mrs.
Hilliard, who lived two houses down, was at
our kitchen door.

"Where in the world did you get those flowers?" she asked Mother. "I've never seen anything like them."

"Aren't they delightful? I'm very pleased with them," said Mother, avoiding Mrs. Hilliard's question.

"Is it something in the soil?" demanded my friend Margie's father, who came by after supper. "Some chemical? Good mulch?"

"You might say a secret ingredient," said Mother, putting an arm around Hilary.

But the neighbor who concerned me most was old Mr. Rush down the street. "There's a magic in those flowers," he complained, "that I just can't put my finger on. But don't think I'm going to stop trying."

Could he connect up Hilary and the garden? Would he? It was hard to see how, but for the next week, no one in our family uttered the word "fairy." I even took the trash out the old way and Mother emptied the dishwasher by hand, the way we had before Hilary brought magic to our house.

But Mr. Rush still kept coming by on sunny days to stand on the sidewalk and stare at the garden. And Hilary and I, our pleasure in the bright weather dimmed by worry, asked ourselves over and over again the same two questions.

Could he? Would he?

9

Where's Hilary?

"Mother, have you seen Hilary?"

I poked my head into the living room, where Mother was at the desk putting stamps on a pile of envelopes.

She shook her head. "Not for a half hour or so. Last I saw her, she went upstairs to put calamine on her mosquito bites. I thought she was outside with you."

I shook my head. "We were cleaning our bikes, and she said she was going to come back to finish. But then she never did."

"Well, she can't be far. Why don't you go see if she's in your bedroom?"

I ran up the stairs, but Hilary wasn't in our bedroom. She wasn't anywhere downstairs either.

"Might she have gone back out and you just didn't see her?" asked Mother when I came back into the living room.

"I guess," I said doubtfully. I ran to the kitchen door and yelled "Hilary! HILARY!" No one answered.

"That's odd," said Mother, frowning. "Let me go upstairs and look one more time."

"I'll go see if she's in the yard."

I looked all around outside. I checked the tree Hilary liked to climb and the spot behind the garage where we'd been trying to start a worm farm. I even looked under the tarp Daddy used to cover the wheelbarrow, in case Hilary was hiding there. But why would she hide from us?

"Hilary, where *are* you?" I called, walking down the driveway and out to the sidewalk. "Hil-a-ry?" Even I could hear the alarm now creeping into my voice.

Mrs. Upchurch across the street was sweeping her front walk.

"Something wrong, Caroline?"

"I'm just looking for Hilary," I told her. "You haven't seen her, have you?"

"Not today, I don't think. Should I send her home if she comes by?"

"Please," I told her. "Right away."

"Hilary, did you say?" said Mr. Rush, appearing suddenly behind me. "Is Hilary missing?"

"She's not *missing*," I said shortly, suddenly wanting to get back home to my mother. "We just can't find her."

Mother was waiting as I raced up the

kitchen steps. "You didn't find her," she said.

I shook my head.

"I don't understand it," Mother said. "We were going to play Uno before dinner. She's been pestering me all day."

The front door closed with a bang. "There she is now," I said with relief. "Hilary! We're in the kitchen!"

"Who's in the kitchen?" said Daddy, putting down his briefcase and giving Mother and me each a kiss. "What's for dinner? Where's Hilary?"

As soon as he heard Hilary was missing, Daddy went right back out to drive around and look for her. Mother and I did some telephoning. But none of us had any luck.

"I don't understand," Mother said for the hundredth time as we sat back down at the kitchen table to think. "Where could she be? It's not like her just to disappear."

Then Mother realized what she had said.

"Oh, dear," she whispered. "Oh, no."

"She wouldn't, Mom," I reassured her. "She even once promised me she wouldn't go without telling us. Unless—" I hesitated even saying this "—do you think maybe someone guessed who she was? And then she *had* to go?"

"Like who? Mr. Rush?" Mother asked.

I nodded miserably. "Or Alfonso, maybe, or one of my friends at Susie's birthday party." Or Corky or Brian or the investigators, I added to myself, but Hilary and I had never told Mother and Daddy about *them*.

"Does guessing count?" asked Daddy.

"I don't know," I confessed. "I know mistakes do. That's why Hilary was so scared that time at school with King Arthur."

We all fell silent for a moment.

"Well, we know none of us has said anything," Daddy said, breaking the silence. "And I trust, Caroline, that you and Hilary haven't been up to any shenanigans lately?"

"We haven't done a thing," I told him. "You wouldn't believe how good we've been. And I know King Arthur hasn't said anything either, have you?" I said, reaching down to stroke Arthur, who was keeping a watchful eye on the door.

"Let me go around the block a few more times to see what I can see," Daddy said abruptly, getting up from the table.

Mother didn't want me too far from the house, so I sat down on the side steps to wait for Daddy. Mother clattered around the kitchen for a few minutes, then came out to sit with me.

I pulled her arm around me.

"When Hilary—you know—goes away," I said, leaning into the comfort of her body, "where does she go away *to*?"

"I'm not sure that question has an answer, Caroline."

"I thought I knew Hilary really well. But there's a lot we don't know about her, isn't there?"

"I'm afraid there is."

"But we know she cares about us. And she'd never worry us like this on purpose. I'm sure she wouldn't!"

"I know," said Mother. "That's what worries me."

"Any word?" called Daddy, pulling into the driveway.

Daddy had gone all the way to the school

and hadn't been able to find a trace of Hilary.

"She's nowhere," he said, getting out of the car without even bothering to return it to the garage. "I stopped some joggers and asked them, and some dog walkers. Maybe we should call the police."

"The police!" I looked at my father, aghast. "But they'll start asking who Hilary is and where we got her and things like that. And if we tell them, she'll *have* to disappear! We'll never see her again!"

Daddy ran a hand over his forehead and sighed deeply. "I don't see what choice we have," he said. "If a child's missing—whatever kind of child—I think we have to do everything we can to find her. And I don't know what more we can do now on our own."

"But Hilary's not a regular child—she's a fairy! You know what the rules are!"

"Now, Caroline—"

"Why don't we go and eat first?" Mother said quietly. "If Hilary doesn't come back by the time supper's over, it'll be time enough then to call the police."

No one was in the mood for a real meal, so Mother put her casserole back in the refrigerator, and Daddy made sandwiches instead. I pulled mine apart, and Daddy kept picking his up and putting it down without taking a bite. Finally he pushed his plate away and turned to me.

"Would you please get me a picture of Hilary?" he said. "A photo? Something we can give the police to help them find her."

"But Daddy—"

"I need a photo, Caroline!"

I went upstairs to get our last-day-of-school photos and handed the packet to Daddy without a word. He flipped through the pictures. "Where's Hilary?" he asked me. "These are all just of you."

"But we were standing right next to each other when Mother took them," I said. "Hilary *has* to be in them!" I leaned over to look. There I was in front of the tree where Mother had posed us, but there was no Hilary next to me. Her image had disappeared from every single one of the pictures.

"Oh, no," I moaned. If this was Hilary's idea of a joke, I didn't think it was the least bit funny.

Mother put her arm around me. Daddy looked out helplessly into the deepening shadows.

"What do we do now?" I whispered.

"I don't know," said Daddy, shaking his head.

Suddenly Arthur, at his post by the door, jerked his head up, and the fur stood up on the back of his neck. At the same time, a petal soft breeze brushed my cheek—the same extraordinary breeze I'd noticed that first wonderful day in the car.

"Is it time for dinner?" a familiar voice said, and Hilary appeared in the kitchen, not far from the table. She glanced toward the window and turned to Mother, puzzled. "Why is it dark so early?" she asked.

"Early?" I shouted. "It's almost half past eight. Where have you been? You scared us half to death!"

Hilary looked hurt. "What did I do?" she asked Mother and Daddy.

"Look at the time, Hilary," Mother said. "We've been searching the neighborhood for you since about five. We were just about to go to the police. Where on earth have you been?"

"Oh, dear," said Hilary, her eyes growing wide. "I forgot. Really, I thought I was just going for a minute or two."

"Going where?" said Daddy, frowning.

"Home," Hilary confessed. "Just for a quick

visit. But time is different in fairyland. That's why even though I was there only a few minutes, a lot more time went by here while I was gone. I'm really sorry I worried you."

Daddy cleared his throat noisily. "Well, no harm done, I guess," he said. "Now that you're back."

Mother gave Hilary a sandwich, and a piece of chocolate cake for dessert. She and Daddy started on the dishes while I kept Hilary company at the table. I was so glad to see her that I kept patting her arm while she ate. Fairyland, I kept thinking. Hilary's been in fairyland!

"What was it like being in fairyland?" I asked Hilary wonderingly. "I bet you're sorry you're back."

"They don't have your mother's chocolate cake in fairyland," Hilary said with her mouth full.

Daddy smiled at her.

"Can you still stay with us then?" I asked her.

"Yes, Caroline."

"Forever?"

"Not forever, Caroline. You know that."

"But . . ."

"You'll be fine when I leave," Hilary said. "You'll have your mother and dad and King Arthur—"

"But I won't have you!"

When I said that, King Arthur gave a little cry at the back of his throat. Hilary put her fork down. I sniffed in hard. "We didn't even have a picture of you!" I reproached Hilary. "We looked at the photos Mother took, and you'd disappeared right out of them."

"That's because you can't take pictures of fairies."

"But I'll at least *remember* you when you leave for good, won't I?" I asked. I didn't think I could bear knowing Hilary was going to disappear from my mind the way she had from those pictures.

Hilary nodded.

"Always?"

"For as long as you want to," Hilary said, her voice soft.

"That's always, then," I declared fiercely.

An idea occurred to me at that moment

that was almost as wonderful as Hilary's coming to live with our family.

"I know," I told Hilary, jumping up from the table. "I'll write it all down. It'll be a fairy story! You can help me if you want. I'll write about a fairy who comes to live with a family, and she and the girl do magic together, and the whole family loves the fairy a lot. . . ."

Mother crossed the room to drop a kiss on Hilary's head.

"Funny how familiar this sounds," said Daddy, winking at Hilary.

Hilary's eyes were shining.

"I know we can't let anyone else read it," I continued, rummaging through Mother's kitchen drawer for some paper and a pencil. "But that's okay—this way we can put all our adventures in it. Though of course we don't know yet what the ending's going to be. . . ."

"Isn't that what adventure's all about?" said Mother.

"Rrrow," said King Arthur.

"How about a cat?" said Daddy. "Can Arthur be in it?"

"There's always room for a cat," Hilary assured him.

I sat back down at the table and picked up my pencil.

"Ready if you are, Hilary," I said. "Let's get this story under way!"